WILLIAM WORRYDACTYL

First published in 2013 by Wayland

Text copyright © Brian Moses
Illustrations copyright © Mike Gordon

Wayland
338 Euston Road
London NW1 3BH

Wayland Australia
Level 17/207 Kent Street
Sydney, NSW 2000

Senior editor: Victoria Brooker
Creative design: Basement68
Digital colour: Molly Hahn

British Library Cataloguing
in Publication Data:

Moses, Brian, 1950-
  William Worrydactyl. --
  (Dinosaurs have feelings, too)
  1. Children's stories--Pictorial
  works.
  I. Title II. Series III. Gordon, Mike,
  1948 Mar. 16-
  823.9'2-dc23
ISBN: 978 0 7502 7115 8

Printed in China

Wayland is a division of
Hachette Children's Books,
an Hachette UK company.
www.hachette.co.uk

WiLLiAM WORRYDACTYL

Written by
Brian Moses

Illustrated by
Mike Gordon

WORRIES

WAYLAND

William Worrydactyl lived
in a very tall tower.

His Mum and Dad
would fly out of the
window when they
left home.

But William was too
worried to fly out
of the window. He
worried that he wouldn't
be able to fly, or land.

When his parents took him out, they all went down in the lift.

But William worried about being in a lift.

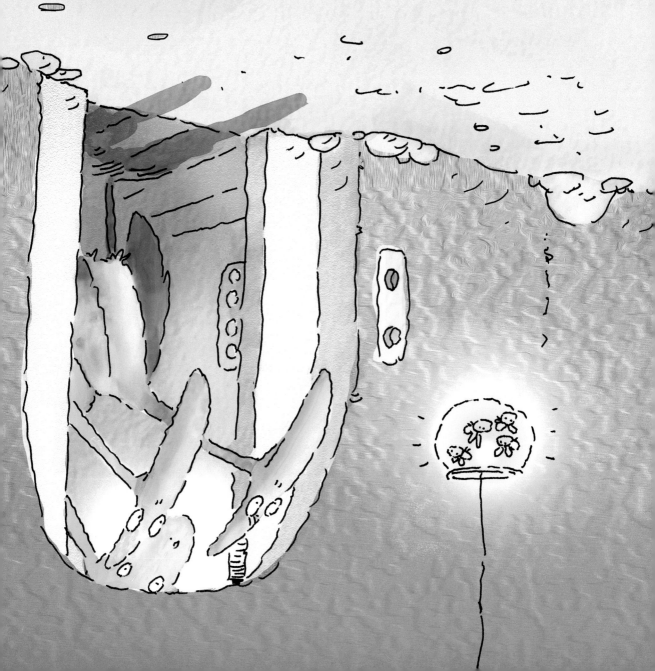

He worried about getting his wings
trapped in the door when it closed.

William worried that when it got dark at night, it wouldn't get light again the next day.

William worried that his
wings weren't as strong
as his friends' wings.

He worried that he
couldn't jump as high
as they could.

He worried about going to flying dino-school.

William didn't seem
able to learn to fly like
the other dinosaurs.

"Everyone worries a bit," his Mum said.

"But you, William, your worries are like wriggly worms slithering around in your head."

William's Mum made a Worry Box. "You can write down your worries on little pieces of paper and put them into this box," she said.

"Then we'll take out a different worry each night and talk about it before you go to sleep."

So that's what William did. He wrote down his worries; his big worries and his little worries.

20

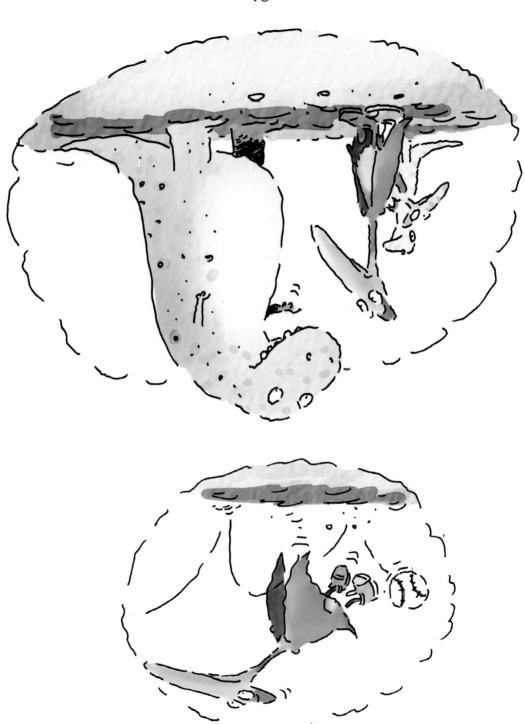

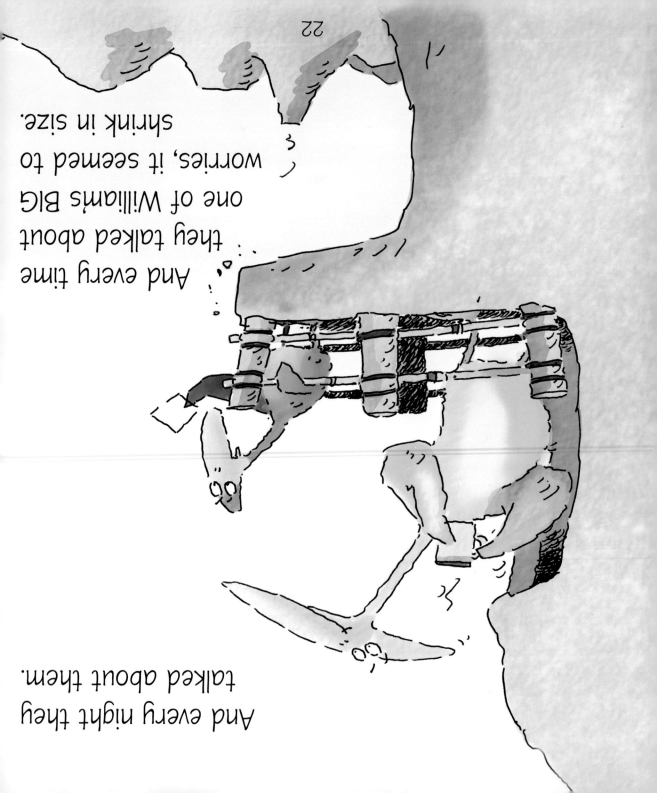

And every time
they talked about
one of William's BIG
worries, it seemed to
shrink in size.

And every night they
talked about them.

And every time they talked about one of Williams little worries, it seemed to disappear.

Until one day William said, "If I want to see my worries now, I think I'll need a magnifying glass."

"I think the time has come for
me to try my first flight."

As William stood at the window ready
to take off, his Mum warned him, "Be careful."

While his Dad called out,
"Only a short one."

And he was...

NOTES FOR PARENTS AND TEACHERS

Read the book with children either individually or in groups. Talk to them about what makes them worried? How do they feel when they are worried?

Focus on a worry that a child has had in the past but has now been resolved. What was the occasion and the outcome? Can this be used as a basis for a story about worrying? The story could have three parts: a) the reason for worrying, b) the event that caused the worry, c) the aftermath of the event.

Alternatively help children to compose short poems that focus on their own worries:

I worry about my ballet exams. Will I do as well as I should?
I worry about learning my spelling. Will I get them right?
I worry about my sister when she's unwell. I hope she's better soon.
I worry about...etc.

Poems could also be written looking at other people's worries:

My Dad worries about his garden. Will the slugs eat his cabbages this year?
My teacher worries about her class. Will the children learn as much as they should?

This can lead to a discussion about ways in which worries can be overcome. Do children have any ways of dealing with worries that they have found helpful to them? What can be done to remove the source of a worry?

Point out to children that their parents worry about them, just like Williams parents worried about him when he was about to make his first flight. Do children know what worries their parents have about them?

My Mum always worries that I haven't put enough warm clothes on when I go outside in the winter.
My Dad always worries about me hurting myself when I use one of his tools.

Can children think of other words that describe how worried we can be, such as 'nervous', 'anxious', 'tense', 'stressed', 'dismayed', 'uneasy', 'fretful', 'agitated', 'distressed'.

Some children might like to make their own 'worry boxes' and do what William did each evening.

Explore 'worrying' further through the sharing of picture books mentioned on page 32. Talk to children about their worries and reassure them that it is natural to worry and that everyone worries from time to time.

BOOKS TO SHARE

I'm Worried (Your Feelings) by Brian Moses (Wayland, 1998)
Looks at what children worry about and how they can
overcome their worries.

Morris & the Bundle of Worries by Jill Seeney, illustrated by
Rachel Fuller. (British Association for Adoption and Fostering, 2007)
Well-written story about learning how to deal with,
and manage, worries.

Mr Worry (Mr. Men Classic Library) by Roger Hargreaves
(Egmont Books, 2008)
This series has been around for a while now, but children
love these characters.

Silly Billy by Anthony Browne (Walker Books, 2007)
Billy is a bit of a worrier. Find out how he overcomes his worry
about staying at other people's houses with the aid of
some worry dolls.

The Huge Bag of Worries by Virginia Ironside,
illustrated by Frank Rodgers
(Hodder Childrens' Books, 2011)
Jenny's worries follow her wherever
she goes – in a big blue bag! Who can
she get to help her get rid of her worries?
A reassuring read.

Titles in the series:

Anna Angrysaurus
9780750271112

Gracie Grumposaurus
9780750271141

Jamal Jealousaurus
9780750271165

Samuel Scaredosaurus
9780750271134

Sophie Shyosaurus
9780750271172

William Worrydactyl
9780750271158

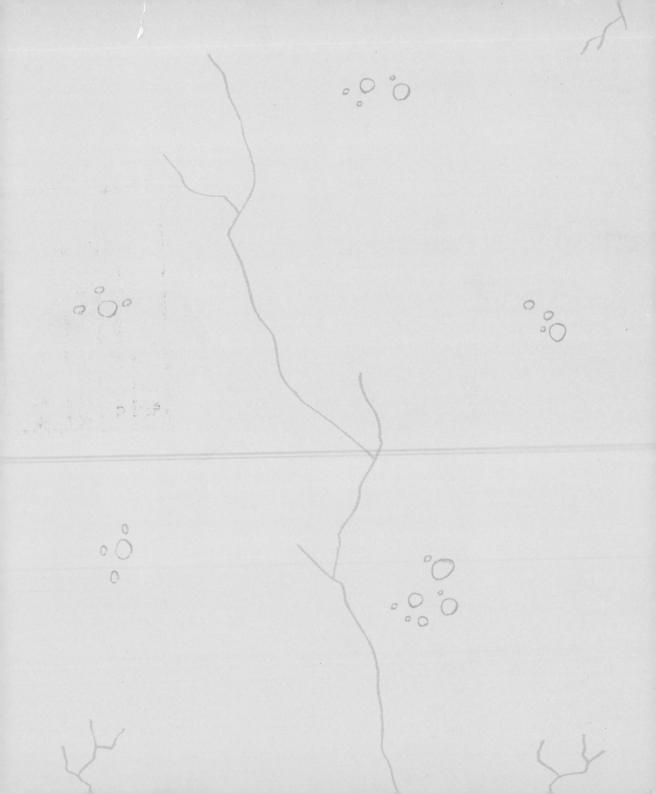